Dear Moon Baby

By *Andrew Davenport*

Copyright © 2020 Moon and Me

Scholastic Children's Books,
Euston House, 24 Eversholt Street,
London NW1 1DB, UK

A division of Scholastic Ltd
London ~ New York ~ Toronto ~ Sydney ~ Auckland
Mexico City ~ New Delhi ~ Hong Kong

Published in the UK by Scholastic Ltd, 2020

ISBN 978 14071 9814 9

Printed in China

2 4 6 8 10 9 7 5 3 1

The right of Andrew Davenport to be identified as the author of this work respectively has been asserted by him in accordance with the Copyright, Designs and Patents Act, 1988.

Papers used by Scholastic Children's Books are made from wood grown in sustainable forests.

www.scholastic.co.uk

Lambkin

Lily Plant

Colly Wobble

Moon Baby

Little Nana

Dibillo

Pepi Nana

Mr Onion

3

A Letter to the Moon!

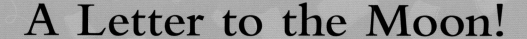

Once upon a time, there was a magical toy that came to life whenever the moon shone.

Her name was Pepi Nana.

"Tiddle toddle!"

Pepi Nana likes to write letters.

"**Tiddle toddle!**" she said. "I will write a letter to the moon!"

So, she did.

What a good idea, Pepi Nana!

Away went the tiny letter, to the moon.

Pepi Nana didn't know that on the moon lived Moon Baby.

"This letter is for Moon Baby!" thought Moon Baby.

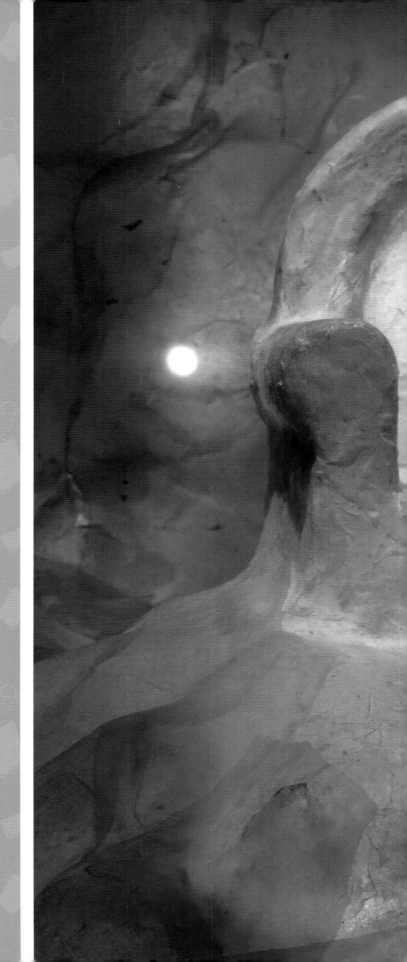

Moon Baby wanted to visit Pepi Nana, very much.

He pulled up his hood …   Put on his gloves …

And Moon Baby flew all the way down from the moon.

"Tiddle toddle!"
said Pepi Nana.
"My new friend,
Moon Baby!"

Pepi Nana and
Moon Baby are
happy friends,
together.

And all because of
Pepi Nana's letter!

A Letter to Everybody!

Inside the little Toy House, everybody was very busy.

Washing up the cups and saucers…

…laying the table…

…making
the beds…

…and tidying
the books.

Pepi Nana was very happy to be with her friends.

"**Tiddle toddle!**" she said. "I will write a letter. To everybody!"

So, she did.

What a good idea, Pepi Nana!

Pepi Nana wrote a very special letter.

Pepi Nana's friends were very happy, together.

And all because of Pepi Nana's letter!

A Letter to Moon Baby!

Once upon a time, Pepi Nana wanted to ride on the tricycle-made-for-two with her friend Moon Baby.

"Tiddle toddle!" she said. **"I will write a letter to Moon Baby!"**

So, she did.

What a good idea, Pepi Nana!

Pepi Nana drew a picture of the tricycle-made-for-two.

"This letter is for Moon Baby," said Pepi Nana.

Pepi Nana gave her letter to Colly Wobble, to deliver in the car.

Colly Wobble gave the letter to Mr Onion, to deliver in the bumparoller.

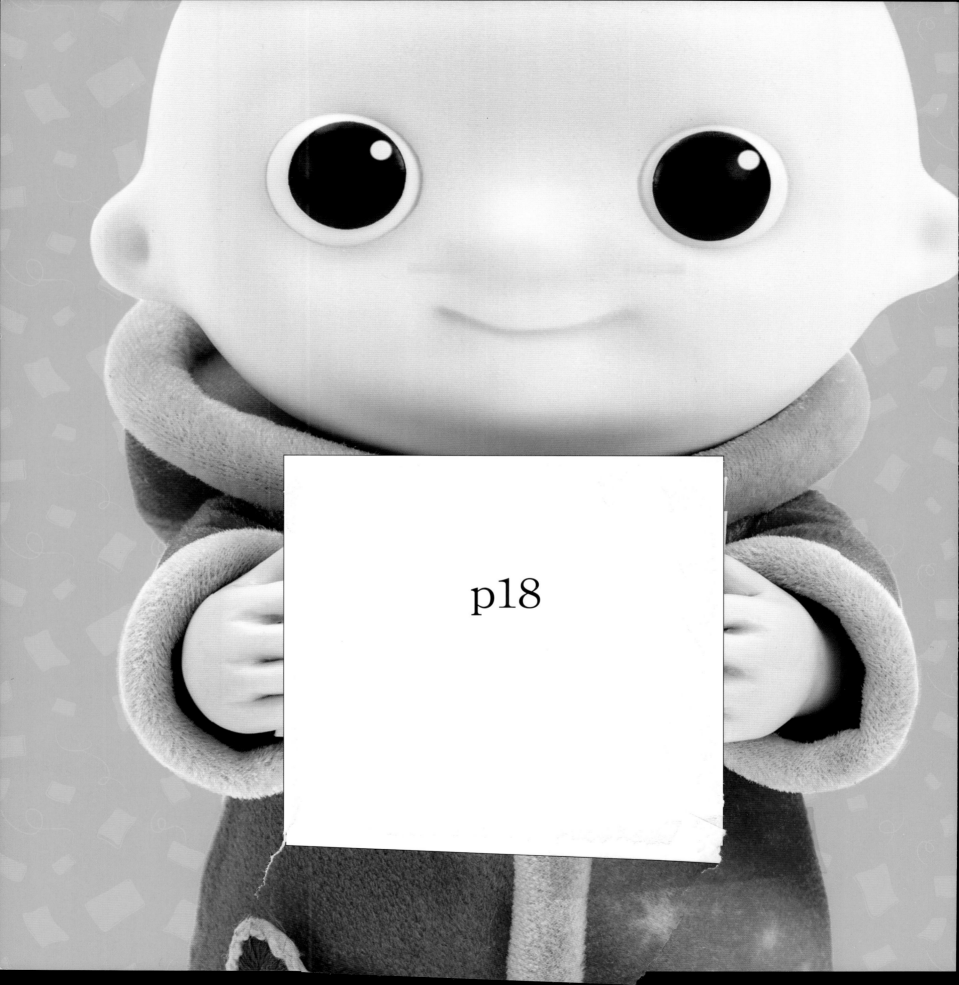

Mr Onion gave the letter to Dibillo, to deliver in the balloon.

Dibillo gave the letter to Little Nana and Lambkin, to deliver in the aeroplane.

And Little Nana and Lambkin delivered the letter to Moon Baby.

"**This letter is for Moon Baby!**"
thought Moon Baby.

And he opened Pepi Nana's letter.

Moon Baby liked Pepi
Nana's picture of the
tricycle-made-for-two.

He went to see Pepi Nana,
as fast as he could.

Pepi Nana and Moon Baby
rode on the tricycle-made-for-two.

Dring, dring!

What fun they had, together.

And all because of Pepi Nana's letter!

A Special Letter!

"Hush, hush," says the Moon,
"it's time to go to sleep."

"Tiddle toddle!"
said Pepi Nana.
"I will leave a
special letter on
my table, all
ready to write!"

So, she did.

What a good idea,
Pepi Nana!

Now you can write a special letter.

And who knows what might happen, next time Moon Baby comes to visit.

And all because of your letter!

Goodnight,
Pepi Nana.

Goodnight,
Moon Baby.